Ever After High™

GENERAL VILLAINY

A DESTINY DO-OVER DIARY

THIS BOOK
BELONGS TO

EVER AFTER
Royals!

EVER AFTER
Rebels

GENERAL VILLAINY

A DESTINY DO-OVER DIARY

Suzanne Selfors

LITTLE, BROWN AND COMPANY

New York   Boston

Little, Brown and Company
Hachette Book Group
1290 Avenue of the Americas, New York, NY 10104
Visit us at lb-kids.com

Little, Brown and Company is a division of Hachette Book Group, Inc.
The Little, Brown name and logo are trademarks of Hachette Book Group, Inc.

The publisher is not responsible for websites (or their content)
that are not owned by the publisher.

First Edition: January 2015

Library of Congress Control Number: 2014950252

ISBN 978-0-316-40126-5

10 9 8 7 6 5 4 3 2 1

RRD-C

Printed in the United States of America

For Lynn Brunelle,
whose creativity
helped fuel this book

FIG 1. — *The Cauldron*

→ LETTER TO STUDENTS ←

Welcome to General Villainy.

My name is Mr. Badwolf, and I will be your teacher for this class. You should all be familiar with my family's reputation for terrorizing little pigs and grandmothers. I am proud of my villainous bloodline and expect that each of you is equally proud of your heritage.

Because this is an introductory class, you are not expected to have completed a successful evil spree. However, you are expected to understand the difference between good and evil.

If you pass this class, you will be enrolled in Pre-Advanced Villainy, then Advanced Villainy, then Complex Villainy, and, finally, Superior Villainy. You can then select your area of study. For example, some Superior Villainy students choose to major in Worldwide Pandemonium, while others choose to narrow their focus to Township Terror or Castle Chaos.

There are rules that must be followed at all times while attending my class. The rules list is included on the next page.

I look forward to teaching you this year, and hopefully, under my guidance, your mean, rotten, and nasty sides will shine!

Respectfully yours,

MR. BADWOLF

GENERAL VILLAINY CLASSROOM RULES

1. PROPER CLOTHING MUST BE WORN.

Clothing should be dark and serious.

Black is preferred, followed by somber gray. Depressing, muddy colors are acceptable. Pink and lavender will not be tolerated. And FYI, pastel colors are NOT evil, nor is anything floral or polka-dotted.

Capes are always fun!

2. GUM-CHEWING IS PROHIBITED.

I do not want to waste time trying to get gum out of my luxurious fur—I mean, my hair! So anyone chewing gum in class will receive dungeon detention.

Of course, if you choose to dispose of your gum in someone else's hair or fur, then that would be very evil and you will receive hextra credit.

3. CHEATING IS ALLOWED AND EXPECTED.

Reading over someone's shoulder and copying answers is a hexcellent way to cheat, as is stealing your roommate's thronework.

4. DISRUPTION IS WELCOME.

Please feel free to interrupt and annoy your fellow students. But don't try any of that on me or I will send you to dungeon detention.

5. GO TO BED EARLY.

Creating chaos can be exhausting for the beginning student. Nutritious food and good sleep will keep you healthy and ready to unleash your wickedness.

Of course, causing others to lose sleep is very evil indeed and will earn you hextra credit.

LIZZIE'S ALARM CLOCK

According to Mr. Badwolf's rules list, every villain needs a good night's sleep. But while the other General Villainy students have alarms that wake them up in the morning so they can get to class on time, Lizzie Hearts doesn't have one.

Can you think about the things that Lizzie likes and create a clock for her? Remember that Lizzie is from Wonderland. She loves to play croquet, she has a pet hedgehog named Shuffle, and her mother is the Queen of Hearts. Is her alarm clock heart-shaped? Hedgehog-shaped? Use your hexcellent imagination.

BIRDS OF A FEATHER FLOCK TOGETHER

Duchess Swan often uses this phrase, especially when she's talking about the royal princesses. It means that people who are similar, or who have the same interests, usually hang out together. This happens in high school when students form clubs.

Some of the clubs at Ever After High include the Peas Porridge Hot Club and the Rebel Support Group. The students from Wonderland have formed the Croquet Team, and some of the Royals belong to the Tiara and Crown Collectors Club.

EVER AFTER Rebels

Royals!

Can you create some new clubs for Ever After High?
Make one that only Royals would belong to. Make
another just for the Rebels. Be sure to create a club
that Duchess would like, and one for Lizzie, too.

List:

Think of a club at your school that is based on an interest. For example, the Comic Book Club.

Now make up some new clubs for your school. They can be based on interests, attitudes, or anything you want. Be sure to create a few that you'd like to belong to.

List:

Now write a story about one of these clubs. Who is the leader? Do the members sit together at lunch? Do they dress the same? Are they welcoming or exclusive? Are you a member or maybe even the president of the club?

OH CURSES!

Thanks to a curse in her family's past, Duchess Swan's destiny is to spend her life in the form of a swan.

Pretend that you've been cursed to spend your days in animal form. Which animal would you choose to be? Draw a picture of your transformation.

OH CURSES! THE STORY

Now write a story about your transformation.
Think about the following things: Do you hide
or do you show everyone your transformed self?
Do you go to school? How do you get there?
How do you communicate with your friends?
Do they believe that you can become an animal?

LIZZIE'S LACKEYS

Lizzie Hearts's mother, the Queen of Hearts, has an entire army of cards at her disposal. Lizzie doesn't, though—that's why her dorm room is such a mess! So why not create an entourage to help her with her daily chores?

What should their uniforms look like? Should the cards wear hats? Don't forget that the heart symbol is super-important to Lizzie.

LIZZIE'S DESTINY DO-OVER

Lizzie Hearts's destiny is to become the next Queen of Hearts. Her mother ruled with a hot temper, and everyone expects Lizzie to do the same. But Lizzie is torn between her duty to follow in her mother's angry footsteps and her natural desire to rule with a gentler hand.

Can you imagine Lizzie's dilemma? On one hand, she feels the pressure to live up to hexpectations, but on the other, she simply wants to be herself.

If you could be Lizzie for one day, what would you write in your diary? How would you like things to be different when you become queen?

GENERAL ✳ VILLAINY

Dear Diary,

RIDDLE ME THIS

Lizzie Hearts and the other students from Wonderland speak Riddlish, a mysterious language that uses riddles. If Lizzie wanted to keep her plan for her General Villainy thronework a secret, she could write it in Riddlish and most of the students at Ever After High wouldn't be able to understand it. Riddles are fun and tricky at the same time. Can you solve the following riddles?

1. Take off my skin—I won't cry, but you will! What am I?

2. No sooner spoken than broken. What is it?

3. Some months have thirty days; some months have thirty-one days. How many have twenty-eight?

4. The more you have of this, the less you see.

5. The more it dries, the wetter it gets.

Answers: 1. an onion, 2. silence, 3. all of them, 4. darkness, 5. a towel

THE WORST DAY NEVER AFTER!

Duchess Swan is embarrassed when she gushes over Daring Charming. If only she could rewrite her day.

Your worst day ever doesn't have to be the worst day never after! Write your most embarrassing moment and then flip the script and write it the way you wish it turned out.

DUCHESS'S DESTINY DO-OVER

Duchess Swan is envious when Daring Charming asks Lizzie out on a date. As far as Duchess knows, there is no Prince Charming written into her destiny. She is destined to be a princess, but never a queen.

Can you create a new story for Duchess, one that includes Daring Charming or another fairytale prince?

Or maybe Duchess decides she doesn't want a prince in her future. Maybe her pet swan, Pirouette, and her ballet dancing are more important to her. What fableous things are in store for her?

RE
Write

GENERAL VILLAINY QUIZ #1

DO YOU KNOW YOUR EVIL HISTORY? PART 1.

Mr. Badwolf has a quiz for his General Villainy students.

DRAW A LINE AND MATCH THE VILLAINS
WITH THEIR DASTARDLY DEEDS.

1. the Evil Queen

2. the Evil Stepmother

3. Queen of Hearts

4. Mr. Badwolf

5. the Candy Witch

6. the Fox and the Cat

7. the Sheriff of Nottingham

8. the Beanstalk Giant

a. tried to steal gold coins from Pinocchio

b. built a house of sweets to lure hungry children

c. captured Robin Hood

d. imprisoned the Singing Harp

e. poisoned an apple and gave it to Snow White, then took over several other kingdoms

f. made Cinderella do the dishes

g. growled at a sweet little old lady

h. arrested Alice and put her on trial

Answers: 1. *e,* 2. *f,* 3. *h,* 4. *g,* 5. *b,* 6. *a,* 7. *c,* 8. *d*

GENERAL VILLAINY QUIZ #2

DO YOU KNOW YOUR EVIL HISTORY?
PART 2.

Mr. Badwolf is having his neck and back hair trimmed at the Tower Hair Salon in the Village of Book End, so it would be fableous if you could create this quiz for him. Write in some villains and heroes who battled (mix them up!), and create an answer key at the bottom.

Try the quiz out on a friend!

MATCH THE FAIRYTALE VILLAINS
WITH THE HEROES WHO OUTWIT THEM.

Villains	Heroes
1.	a.
2.	b.
3.	c.
4.	d.
5.	e.
6.	f.
7.	g.
8.	h.

DUCHESS SWAN
WORD SEARCH

Look for these words in the puzzle—can you
find them all? Words may appear up, down,
across, backward, or diagonally!

PIROUETTE   HONK

ROYAL   TRUMPETER

BLACK SWAN   GRACEFUL

CYGNETS   PRINCESSOLOGY

SHUFFLE   PAS DE DEUX

BALLET   PRINCE

NEST

```
P R R X J N T B L B N E D
T R J Y K B A U L N T V Y
R L I T G L F A V T L X N
U D Y N L E C E E R U G C
M J R E C K L U C E G Y T
P J T A S E O F D N G Q P
E L R W N R S E F N I T R
T G A T I E D S E U L R T
E N R P D S S T O Y H L P
R N O L A G S T K L J S P
Q M Y P P L Y N P Y O Y Z
M J A W Q N O P K L Y G R
L Z L N P H N Y Y T Q B Y
```

THE EVIL-NAME GAME

⇥ LETTER TO STUDENTS ⇤

Dear General Villainy students,

If you succeed in this class, you will be on the right path to embracing your destiny to become a villain. It's never too early to start thinking about your villain name. Here's a game you can play to help you with this task.

Respectfully yours,

MR. BADWOLF

EVIL NAMES FOR GIRLS

Roll a die three times to discover your new name.
For example, rolls of 6, 1, and 4 make you Sorceress
Villainessa.

Roll 1	Roll 2	Roll 3
1: Lady	1: Villain	1: ella
2: Princess	2: Rotten	2: asha
3: Dr.	3: Evil	3: olly
4: Queen	4: Terror	4: essa
5: Commander	5: Bad	5: illy
6: Sorceress	6: Mean	6: y

Not happy with the results? Create your own evil-name game.

Roll 1

1:_____

2:_____

3:_____

4:_____

5:_____

6:_____

Roll 2

1:_____

2:_____

3:_____

4:_____

5:_____

6:_____

Roll 3

1:_____

2:_____

3:_____

4:_____

5:_____

6:_____

EVIL NAMES FOR BOYS

Roll a die twice to discover your new evil name.
For example, rolls of 1 and 6 make you Mr. Chaos.

Roll 1

1: Mr.

2: Dr.

3: Son of

4: Commander

5: Prince

6: King

Roll 2

1: Bob

2: Cranky

3: Danger

4: Crooked

5: Mad

6: Chaos

Not happy with the results? Create your own evil-name game.

Roll 1

1: _____

2: _____

3: _____

4: _____

5: _____

6: _____

Roll 2

1: _____

2: _____

3: _____

4: _____

5: _____

6: _____

SPARROW'S DESTINY DO-OVER

Sparrow Hood is one of the students at Ever After High who doesn't care about his destiny. He's chosen to follow his own path—to become a singer-songwriter.

Robin Hood, Sparrow's famous dad, doesn't understand why his son isn't spending his days robbing from the rich and giving to the poor. Music seems like such a waste of time. Can you create a conversation between Sparrow and his dad?

What does Sparrow say to his father?

HEXPECTATIONS, SCHMEXPECTATIONS

Raven Queen is in General Villainy class because it is her destiny to become the most evil of all. Everyone believes she will fulfill her role as the next Evil Queen. This stresses her out because she feels a constant pressure to live up to other people's hexpectations.

Do you ever feel this kind of pressure?

When? Why do you feel that way?

Do people expect certain things from you?

What makes you feel they expect them?

Write about the pressures you feel.

You Only Live
Once Upon A Time

Now write about how you would
like to change things.

THE VILLAIN'S DIARY

MR. BADWOLF, AKA THE BIG BAD WOLF

It was supposed to be a day worth spellebrating, for the Big Bad Wolf. Yesterday, he blew down the house of straw, but the three pigs escaped and hid in the house of sticks. Today he was going to blow down the house of sticks. One problem: He woke up with a terrible case of frog-in-throat and is unable to huff and puff.

Can you write his diary entry for the day?

DEAR EVIL DEED DIARY,

DESIGN SOME EVIL UNIFORMS

→ FROM THE HEADMASTER ←

Dear General Villainy students,

The faculty is considering an official evil uniform for all Villainy students to wear to class and to school assemblies. Ms. Faybelle Thorn, daughter of the Dark Fairy in the Sleeping Beauty story, has volunteered to be in charge of this project. Show your school spirit and take pride in being the next generation of evil villains by volunteering to help Ms. Thorn with this project.

Headmaster Grimm

Using markers, colored pencils, or whatever art supplies you like to work with, create an evil school uniform for girls and boys.

GENERAL VILLAINY QUIZ #3

HAVE YOU PERFECTED YOUR EVIL MANNERS? PART 1.

Mr. Badwolf has another pop quiz for his students.
Do you know the answers?

Circle the correct answer to each question:

1. If someone works very hard and builds a new house,
and then invites you for dinner, you should:

  a. bring a lovely housewarming gift such as
    dish towels or candles.

  b. offer to help cook.

  c. show up late, then blow
    the house down!

2. If a girl is born in your kingdom and she is

   prettier than you, you should:

   a. give her something poisonous to eat.

   b. ignore her because true beauty is on the inside.

   c. help her become a supermodel.

3. If you find a frog who claims to be a prince and who

   begs you to kiss him and set him free, you should:

   a. kindly tell him you are allergic to amphibians,
   but that you wish him the best.

   b. kiss him and set him free.

   c. put frog legs on the Castleteria menu!

4. If you decide to steal something, you should:

   a. steal from the rich and give to the poor.

   b. steal from the poor and give to the rich.

   c. steal whatever you want, whenever you want, from
   whomever you want—and keep it all for yourself!

*Answers: If you are wondering whether or not
you answered correctly, then you are not a villain.
Go take the remedial class, Villains 101.*

GENERAL VILLAINY QUIZ #4

HAVE YOU PERFECTED YOUR EVIL MANNERS? PART 2.

Mr. Badwolf has an appointment for his annual rabies shot, but he hasn't finished writing the quiz. If you finish it for him, you'll get hextra credit. Don't forget to fill in the answers at the end.

Circle the correct answer(s):

1. If you meet a nice little wooden boy who has some gold coins, you should:

   a.

   b.

   c.

2. If you see an egg sitting on a wall, and he's minding his own business and seems perfectly happy, you should:

a.

b.

c.

3. If you are not invited to the king and queen's baby shower, you should:

a.

b.

c.

4. If your goody-goody stepsister wants to go to the ball, you should:

a.

b.

c.

Answers: 1. ___, 2. ___, 3. ___, 4. ___.

SHUFFLE'S COSTUME

Lizzie Hearts's pet hedgehog, Shuffle, likes to accompany her to events at Ever After High. Using markers or colored pencils, design two outfits for Shuffle to wear to the following events:

A masquerade ball for villains only

A tea party for Lizzie's birthday

WHAT KIND OF VILLAIN ARE YOU?

Lizzie Hearts struggles with her identity. People hexpect her to be temperamental, just like her mother, the Queen of Hearts. Headmaster Grimm hexpects that Lizzie will do well in General Villainy class. But Lizzie doesn't want to throw tantrums and order people around all the time. She just wants to be nice.

But being nice won't get Lizzie an A in General Villainy.

Answer the following questions and see where you fall in the great scheme of villainy!

1. You can't live without

   a. scheming—being in control is the best.

   b. dreaming—having new ideas is the best.

   c. gleaming—looking good is the best.

2. When it comes to advice,

   a. Mommy knows best.

   b. you don't need any advice ever.

   c. ask a bunch of people and do what works for you.

3. It's better to be

   a. in charge.

   b. correct.

   c. kind.

4. When it comes to friends forever after, it's best to

   a. trick everyone into liking you—popularity
   is power!

   b. have a few close friends whom you trust.

   c. be nice to everyone.

5. Spending time with your BFFA means

   a. making fun of everyone else.

   b. talking and laughing about life.

   c. solving all the problems in the world.

6. You are going to a party and your BFFA has a huge fairy bite (zit) on her chin. What do you do?

  a. Tell her to stay at home until she can find a spell to zap it.

  b. Go anyway—if people are going to be superficial, let them!

  c. Make a joke so you both can laugh—everyone gets fairy bites.

---

7. You're dressing for the Thronecoming Dance.

  a. Be ready in ten minutes—time's wasting!

  b. That takes two hours—everything has to be perfect.

  c. Go out? I have thronework!

---

8. Your favorite sweets from Cooking Class-ic are

  a. ones you can mix sandman powder into.

  b. sweet and gooey cinnamon trolls.

  c. Neither of the above. I'd rather have fresh fruit.

Now add up your answers to discover what kind of villain you are.

Mostly A's
Born to Be Bad

You're in it for yourself. Nobody tells you what to do, and if you were born a villain, you will remain true to villainy! Rock on with your bad self.

Mostly B's
Conflicted Villain

You take chances and you have your head on your shoulders, but when it comes to being a villain, you'd rather not. You have the power and you use it for good.

Mostly C's
Villain FAIL!

You wouldn't know evil if it hit you in the face. And if it did, you would apologize.

LIGHT SIDE/ DARK SIDE

During ballet class, Madame tells Duchess Swan that ballet has a light side and a dark side. She also tells her that each of us has a light side and a dark side.

Do you think that is true? What characteristics do you have that could be categorized as light or dark?

SWAN STYLE

Madame asks Duchess Swan whether she wants to be the prima ballerina and dance the leading role.

Pretend that Pirouette, Duchess's pet swan, has been given the leading role in a ballet.

Design her costume. Use markers or colored pencils to create something fun!

Now she's been invited to a masquerade ball for villains. Design her costume.

NAME THAT EVIL SWAN

Duchess Swan named her pet swan, Pirouette, after one of her favorite ballet moves. But that's such a nice, enchanting name. The Next Top Villain should have a pet with an evil name. Can you help Duchess create a wicked name by taking one word from each column? For example: Princess Crazy Wings. Be sure to fill in the blanks with your own words.

Miss	Rotten	
Queen		Brains
Princess		
Madame	Crazy	Feathers
	Horrid	
Lady		Belch
Señorita	Stinky	Wings
Ms.		Wart
Mademoiselle	Wicked	Feet

RECIPE DO-OVER

Ginger Breadhouse's mother, the Candy Witch, has sent Ginger some of her recipe cards with joke versions of her recipes. (Contrary to her infamous reputation, the Candy Witch never actually cooked any children!) But Ginger has rewritten the recipes.

FROM THE KITCHEN OF:

the Candy Witch

RECIPE:

Boiled kids

DIRECTIONS:

Find kids, stick them in a pot, boil 'em. Yum!

FROM THE KITCHEN OF:

Ginger Breadhouse

RECIPE:

Spoiled Kids

RE Write

DIRECTIONS:

Find kids, stick them in a candy store, let them help themselves. Yum!

Help Ginger change
the following recipes.

FROM THE KITCHEN OF:

the Candy Witch

RECIPE:

Boy Boxed Lunch

DIRECTIONS:

Find a boy, put him between two
slices of bread, stick him in a
lunch box. Enjoy later!

FROM THE KITCHEN OF:

Ginger Breadhouse

RECIPE:

DIRECTIONS:

RE
Write

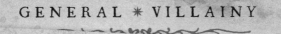
FROM THE KITCHEN OF:

the Candy Witch

RECIPE:

Kid Cobbler

DIRECTIONS:

Get some kids, cover them in piecrust, bake until juicy. Super yummy!

FROM THE KITCHEN OF:

Ginger Breadhouse

RECIPE:

DIRECTIONS:

RE Write

WHITE SWAN/ BLACK SWAN

Duchess Swan is getting ready for a ballet performance. Can you design her white swan costume using markers or colored pencils? Then can you design her black swan costume?

White swan costume:

Black swan costume:

A DESTINY DO-OVER STORY

Duchess Swan and many of the students at Ever After High want to rewrite their destinies. Here's your chance to have fun creating stories for some of the characters.

For each column, roll a die and write down the option next to that number. Then create a story from the pieces. For example, if you roll a 1, a 5, and a 4, write down *Raven Queen*, *the Ballroom*, and *has a crush on someone*. Then write a story using all three elements.

You can do this activity more than once. It will be different every time. Invite your friends to join you, and tell your stories out loud.

Number on the die	Character	Place	Problem
1	Raven Queen	the Enchanted Forest	doesn't remember who he or she is
2	Sparrow Hood	a fancy castle	tries to use magic
3	Faybelle Thorn	the Castleteria	comes up with a wicked plan for General Villainy class
4	Ginger Breadhouse	a royal kingdom	has a crush on someone
5	Duchess Swan	the Ballroom	is in a dream
6	Lizzie Hearts	a gingerbread house	joins a new school club

NOT-SO-POISONED APPLE LIP GLOSS

Raven's got something up her sleeve. When she tried to make a poisoned apple in General Villainy, the apple melted into goop. The goop turned out to not be poisonous, and it made an enchanting apple-scented lip gloss!

Try it!

What you need:

small microwave-safe mixing bowl

4 tablespoons of cocoa butter (*find it at the pharmacy*)

spoon for mixing

3 drops of cinnamon flavoring oil

(*find it at baking specialty stores or online*)

4 drops of apple flavoring oil

1 teaspoon of honey

¼ teaspoon of cooking oil

1 vitamin E capsule

1 small container, lip balm tube, or

small tub with a cap (*find it at a craft store*)

What you do:

1. In a small microwave-safe mixing bowl, melt the cocoa butter in the microwave in five-second intervals. Stir in between. Do not overcook.

2. Add the cinnamon and apple flavoring oil and the honey, and mix well. If it starts to harden while you are mixing, put the bowl in the microwave for five seconds to melt it again.

3. Add the cooking oil.

4. Cut open the vitamin E capsule, and squeeze the substance inside it into the bowl. Stir well.

5. Pour the mixture into a container.

6. Let it cool.

7. Put the cap on.

8. Use it on your lips for a wickedly apple-licious smile!

OFF WITH THEIR HEADS!

Lizzie Hearts's mom, the Queen of Hearts, spends a lot of time ordering her card army to chop off people's heads. She's truly rotten. Here's your chance to do some chopping, but not in a wicked way.

Transform the meaning of the following words by chopping off the first letter to make a new word.

Example: The sound a princess's gown makes becomes something you do when you see a star.

s w i s h / w i s h

1. The place where royal horses sleep becomes a place to eat. _ _ _ _ _ _ / _ _ _ _ _

2. The object you hit in a game of croquet becomes everything. _ _ _ _ / _ _ _

3. The stuff on Lizzie's head becomes the stuff you breathe. _ _ _ _ / _ _ _

4. What Lizzie loves to do with tea becomes a place to skate. _ _ _ _ _ / _ _ _ _

5. The kind of hog that Lizzie loves becomes a boundary. _ _ _ _ _ / _ _ _ _

6. What you do with cards becomes what a chicken does with an egg. _ _ _ _ / _ _ _

95

AN EVIL TRANSFUSION

Raven Queen is in General Villainy class because she has the most evil in her bloodline. Blondie Lockes says that if Raven donated blood, the packet would be labeled TYPE EVIL.

What would Blondie look like if she woke up one morning and found out that her blood was Type Evil? Use colored pencils or markers to create your vision of an evil Blondie.

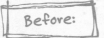

Before:

After:

FRIENDS FOREVER AFTER

In *Next Top Villain*, Duchess Swan has to make a really difficult decision: Should she risk her friendship with her roommate, Lizzie Hearts, just to get a good grade?

How important is friendship to you? Have you ever been in the position where you wanted to do something, but you knew it might hurt a friend's feelings?

Write about it here. Are you happy with the decision you made, or would you like to change it?

You Only Live
Once Upon A Time

EVIL BAKE SALE

Mr. Badwolf has asked the students in General Villainy to hold a bake sale. They need to raise funds to buy more cauldrons. Ginger Breadhouse is in charge, but her treats are way too sweet and charming.

Using markers or colored pencils, can you help Ginger transform her baked delights into evil edibles?

Ginger's cupcake

Evil cupcake

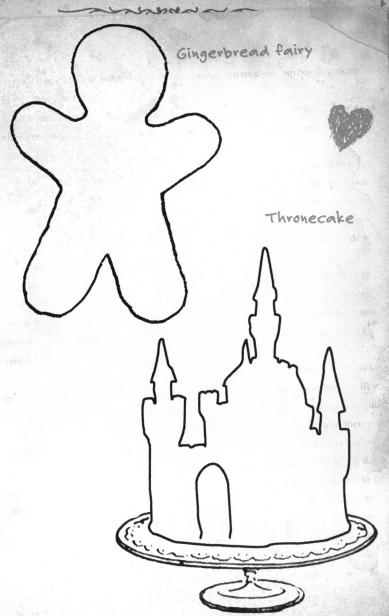

Gingerbread fairy

Thronecake

WRITE YOUR OWN SONG

Stuck in General Villainy class, Sparrow Hood would rather be at his tree house writing music with his band, the Merry Men. Writing lyrics is an art. How do you even start? You have to listen to your own heart and write something rather smart.

Brainstorm ideas.

What is your song about?

    Is it about falling in love? Being misunderstood?

Your favorite pet? A great day? A bad day? What

other people expect of you? Your dreams about

your future?

    Make a list of possible song ideas here:

It's just the beginning Your happily Ever After starts now It's just the beginning Your happily

Create a zippy title.

Why do you need a good title? You want to grab attention. If people find the title interesting, they will listen to the song. If the title falls flat, you might turn people off before they've even given your song a chance. Ideally you want a song title to:

1. Be imaginative (not boring).

2. Be original. Make it something no one has heard before.

3. Be brief. Don't make a title longer than five or six words. People have to be able to remember the title, and they won't if it's really, really long!

4. Make people feel something. You've probably heard a song that made you think, *I get that! I feel that way, too!*

Write down your ideas here:

It's just the beginning. Your happily Ever After starts now. It's just the beginning. Your happily

Write the lyrics.

Now that you have a zippy title and a sense of what your song is about, all you have to do is write it. Sound hard? Not if you take it step-by-step.

Take a look at the pattern of rhyming in your favorite song.

Does every line rhyme? Does it alternate? Or does it even rhyme at all? (A song can be like a poem or a story and not rhyme.)

Here's an example of a lyric Sparrow wrote. The pattern is AABA—that means the first, second, and fourth lines rhyme.

> Take a look and see.
> I own my destiny.
> I rob from the rich
> And give the goods to ME!

It's just the beginning Your happily Ever After starts now It's just the beginning Your happily Eve
Ever After is so Once Upon a Time. Hex Yeah! Hex Yea

Can you write some lyrics in the AABA pattern?

A

A

B

A

A

A

B

A

A

A

B

A

SPARROW'S PLAYLIST

Can you figure out Sparrow Hood's favorite artists? The words have the same meanings. Can you match up the artists with their real names?

Artist

1. Lady Gaga
2. Green Day
3. Pink
4. Fun
5. Queen
6. Coldplay
7. Drake

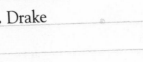

Meaning

a. female monarch

b. amusing time

c. low-temperature stage production

d. environmentally aware period of sunshine

e. male duck

f. not a man and first baby words

g. somewhere between red and white

Answers: 1. f, 2. d, 3. g, 4. b, 5. a, 6. c, 7. e

CHOOSE YOUR MAGIC

The students at Ever After High have different magical abilities. Faybelle Thorn uses her cheers to cast wicked spells, Lizzie Hearts uses her Wonderland cards to build things, and Duchess Swan can transform herself into a swan.

If you could choose one magical ability, what would it be? Write a story in which you show your friends your magic for the first time.

You Only Live
Once Upon A Time

RAVEN'S THEME SONG

As the daughter of a villain, Raven Queen is hexpected to have an evil theme song. If she writes one, she'll get hextra credit in her General Villainy class.

Can you help her write her own song by filling in the blanks? Hint: Raven's lyrics rhyme!

Verse

I'd choose not to be evil if I could.

What I want to be is totally _____.

I feel so trapped in my destiny.

All I want is to be _____.

Chorus

Yeah, yeah, yeah. For me the dark's not right.

Yeah, yeah, yeah. I'm focusing on the _____!

Verse

I sing my fate. I use my voice.

I know deep down I have a _____.

My mom's path was so unkind.

It's time for me to make up my _____.

Chorus

Yeah, yeah, yeah. For me the dark's not right.

Yeah, yeah, yeah. I'm focusing on the _____!

Answers: good, free, light, choice, mind, light

LIZZIE'S MAGIC CARDS

Lizzie Hearts can build all sorts of things out of her magical deck of Wonderland cards.

You don't have to possess a deck of Wonderland cards. You can make an ordinary deck look like magic with the following trick.

What you need:

a deck of cards
salt

What you do:

Before you appear in front of your audience:

1. Find the Queen of Hearts and set it aside.

2. Shuffle the deck of cards.

3. Cut the deck in half and set the halves facedown on the table. Now you have two stacks of cards.

4. Sprinkle some salt on the top of one stack. Do not put salt on the other stack.

5. Now place the Queen of Hearts facedown on top of the salted stack. Place the other stack on top of the Queen of Hearts.

In front of your audience:

1. Ask whether they've heard of the Queen of Hearts. Tell them she is the most powerful card in the deck and that she always wants to be seen.

2. Place the deck on the floor with a flourish.

3. Get someone to gently nudge the deck with a toe to divide it into two piles.

4. Pick up the top pile and show them the card on the bottom.

5. That's right—the Queen of Hearts!

ROYAL MIX-UP

Lizzie Hearts dropped her cards on the floor, and now they're all mixed up. Only three of these queens match. Can you find the one that doesn't?

Now create your own mixed-up cards. Three should match, but the fourth will be slightly different. Can your friends solve your puzzle?

VILLAINY TO-DO LIST

Raven Queen doesn't want to be a villain, so she's having a difficult time in General Villainy class.

Pretend that you want to take Raven's place and become the next Evil Queen.

Can you fill out your daily to-do list for wreaking havoc?

Troublemaking

To-Do List

1. Choose an evil outfit.

2. Have my minions brush and style my hair.

3. Start a food fight in the Castleteria.

4.

5.

6.

7.

8.

9.

10. Go to bed and do it all again tomorrow.

WAIT A SPELL!

Lizzie is usually very skilled at building things with her Wonderland cards, but sometimes things go wrong. This happens to Raven Queen, too. Sometimes she tries to cast spells, but the words backfire.

Here are some examples of Raven's words backfiring. First figure out the word that fits the first clue, and then reverse that word so it fits the second clue.

Example:

Start with another word for *sweet potato*, and end up with a springtime month.

Y A M   M A Y

---

1. Start with what you put on a baby's bottom, and end up with what a debt is after the money has been given back.

＿ ＿ ＿ ＿ ＿   ＿ ＿ ＿ ＿ ＿ ＿

2. Start with what kissing a toad can give you, and end up with what Rumpelstiltskin spins with.

＿ ＿ ＿ ＿ ＿   ＿ ＿ ＿ ＿ ＿

3. Start with another word for *students*, and end up with a mistake.

＿ ＿ ＿ ＿ ＿ ＿

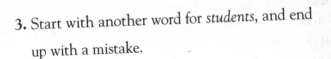

THE EVIL QUEEN

Raven Queen's mother is the infamous Evil Queen.
People say that Raven looks a lot like her mother.

What if you could be the next Evil Queen?
Would you wear a crown? A cape? Can you draw a
picture of what you'd look like?

DREAM YOUR DESTINY

Ginger Breadhouse is the daughter of the Candy Witch. But instead of spending her time being evil, she'd rather cook up sweet treats for everyone to eat, so she chooses to spend her time creating her own delicious concoctions in the Cooking Class-ic kitchen.

We all have the power to shape our own destinies no matter where we come from.

How do you see yourself in the future?
In a year? In five years? In ten years?
Write about it.

It's the first day of high school, and I'm...

Now that I have graduated from high school, I can't wait to...

It's the first day of my first job and...

If I could be remembered for one
thing, it would be...

You Only Live
Once Upon A Time

SPARROW'S GUITAR

If Sparrow Hood is going to succeed in General Villainy, he will need a new look. Can you give his guitar a new, evil design using markers or colored pencils?

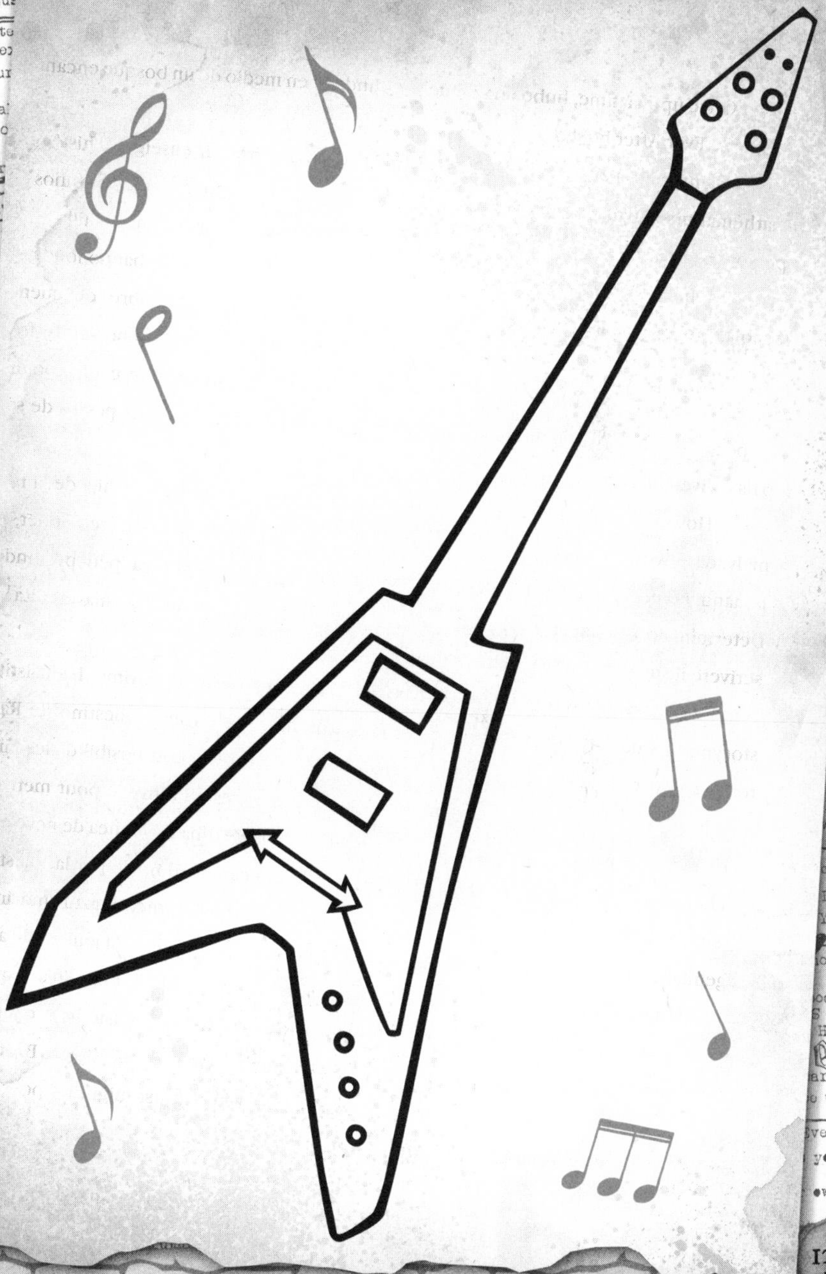

RHYME TIME

Sparrow Hood is chilling out for a spell and not paying attention in General Villainy class. Instead, he's working on some rhymes. Rhyming is an important tool for a songwriter, and Sparrow needs all the practice he can get.

Can you solve his riddles? Hint: The two words rhyme.

1. What do you call it when Hopper Croakington II goes running?

_ _ _ _   _ _ _

2. What do you call it when Lizzie paints a picture?

_ _ _ _ _   _ _ _ _

3. What do you call Raven's mom?

_ _ _ _   _ _ _ _ _

4. What do you call it when Ms. Hearts is feeling loopy?

_ _ _ _ _   _ _ _ _ _

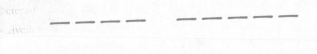

3. mean queen, 4. dizzy Lizzie

Answers: *1. frog jog, 2. heart art*

MIX IT UP

Lizzie Hearts isn't always who she seems. She may yell about having people's heads taken off, but deep down she's a little mixed-up. Mixing things up isn't so bad. . . . It's a great place to start a story.

Choose an item from each column, and then write a story using all three in the first sentence.

For example: On her eightieth birthday, the witch looked out the window of her apartment in Book End.

Character	Age	Location
dragon	one year old	apartment in Book End
prince	five years old	castle
princess	fifteen years old	department store
magic mirror	eighty years old	farm
witch	five hundred years old	school

Write your story here...

GINGER BREADHOUSE WORD SEARCH

Look for these words in the puzzle—can you find them all? Words may appear up, down, across, backward, or diagonally!

RECIPE

SUGAR RUSH

CINNAMON TROLL

THRONECAKE

CUPCAKE CHEF

SWEET DESTINY

SPRINKLES

MIRRORCAST

SANDMAN POWDER

CANDY WITCH

```
S F E K A C E N O R H T D W Y G
A E C A N D Y W I T C H S L T L
N H W Y B J H D B N Z W L S M P
D C Q S L T J S M D E L A J N Q
M E Q Q E N B R U E O C N P M R
A K Y V T L T D T R R B L Y Y Q
N A W D Y D K D T O R E X W R M
P C T D P D E N R M Z A C J P X
O P W B R S O R I Z G K G I D Z
W U Z B T M I N V R L N T U P L
D C L I A M Q Q G T P J P G S E
E X N N W W M Y T J Z S N R L X
R Y N R D Y L T D M Q Y Y B Y R
J I M D R J T P D M R M D R B M
C X Y L D Z R D L D G P V T Q V
```

A FINAL NOTE

Whether a hero or a villain, each student at Ever After High asks the same question—what do I want to do with my life? Do I want to follow the path that others have paved for me, or do I want to find my own way to a Happily Ever After?

Create a destiny do-over for each
of these students:

Ginger Breadhouse

Ginger is destined to become the next Candy Witch,
but Ginger really loves to bake and share her delicious
treats with all the students at Ever After High.
What kind of destiny can you reimagine for her?

RE
Write

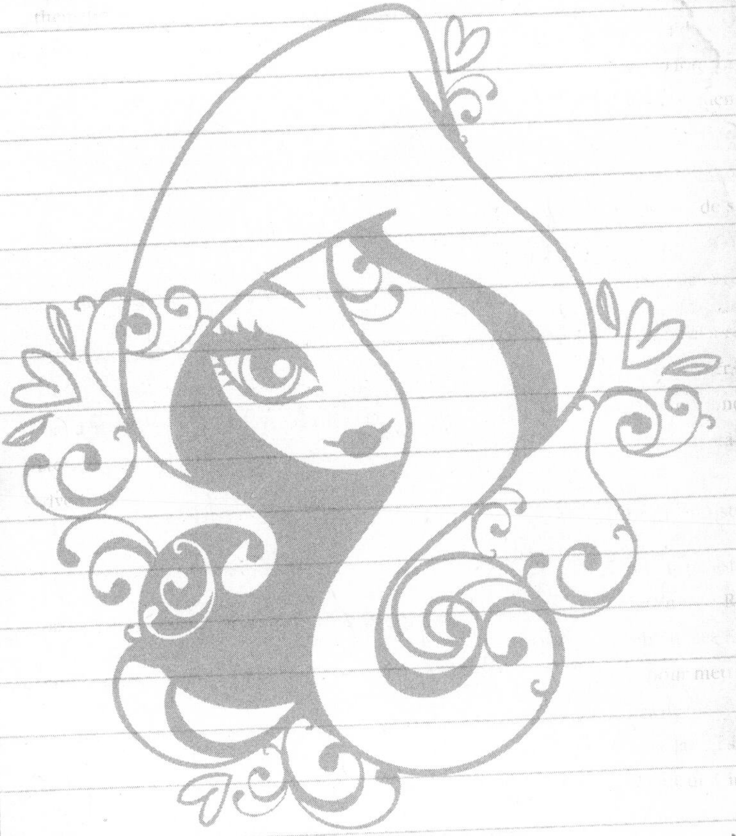

Sparrow Hood

Sparrow is destined to become the next Robin Hood, but Sparrow really wants to write music and play his guitar in a band.

What kind of destiny can you reimagine for him?

RE
Write

RE
Write

Duchess Swan

Duchess is destined to become the next Swan Queen, but she really wants to keep her human legs and dance.

What kind of destiny can you reimagine for her?

You Only Live
Once Upon A Time

Now create a destiny for yourself.

 $\mathcal{D}$ on't miss the novel that goes
with this hextbook!

Read **Next Top Villain** by Suzanne Selfors
to find out what destiny awaits
Duchess Swan and
Lizzie Hearts!